Taaples
Action Rhymes

The Wheels on the Bus

and

The Boat on the Waves

Notes for adults

TADPOLES ACTION RHYMES are structured to provide support for newly independent readers. The books may also be used by adults for sharing with young children.

The language of action rhymes is often already familiar to an emergent reader, so the opportunity to see these rhymes in print gives a highly supportive early reading experience.

The alternative rhymes extend this reading experience further, and encourage children to play with language and try out their own rhymes.

If you are reading this book with a child, here are a few suggestions:

1. Make reading fun! Choose a time to read when you and the child are relaxed and have time to share the story.

2. Recite the rhyme together before you start reading. What might the alternative rhyme be about? Why might the child like it?

3. Encourage the child to reread the rhyme, and to retell it in their own words, using the illustrations to remind them what has happened.

4. Point out together the repeated words on pages 12 and 22 (developing phonological awareness will help with decoding) and encourage the child to make up their own alternative rhymes and accompanying actions.

5. Give praise! Remember that small mistakes need not always be corrected.

First published in 2010 by
Franklin Watts
338 Euston Road
London NW1 3BH

Franklin Watts Australia
Level 17/207 Kent Street
Sydney NSW 2000

Text (Ride, Ride, Ride Your Bike)
© Wes Magee 2010
Illustration © Richard Morgan 2010

The rights of Wes Magee to be identified as the author of Ride, Ride, Ride Your Bike and Marina le Ray as the illustrator of this Work have been asserted in accordance with the Copyright, Designs and Patents Act, 1988.

ISBN 978 0 7496 9367 1 (hbk)
ISBN 978 0 7496 9373 2 (pbk)

The Wheels on the Bus

Retold by Wes Magee
Illustrated by Richard Morgan

FRANKLIN WATTS
LONDON•SYDNEY

**Richard
Morgan**

"I thought it'd be fun to
draw a bus in a tropical
setting, with all the unusual
animals that live there.
Which ones can
you spot?"

The wheels
on the bus go
round and round,

round and round,
round and round.

The wheels on the bus go

round and round,

all day long.

The Wheels on the Bus

The wheels on the bus go

round and round,

round and round,

round and round.

The wheels on the bus go

round and round,

all day long.

Can you point to the repeated words?

The Boat on the Waves

by Wes Magee
Illustrated by Richard Morgan

Wes Magee

"It's exciting to go on a boat trip across the sea. But watch out, the waves going up and down can make you seasick!"

The boat on the waves
goes up and down,

up and down,
up and down.

The boat on the
waves goes
up and down.

Splish! Splash! Splosh!

The Boat on the Waves

The boat on the waves

goes up and down,

up and down,

up and down.

The boat on the waves

goes up and down.

Splish! Splash! Splosh!

Can you point to the repeated words?

Puzzle Time!

How many boats can you
see in this picture?

Answers

There are 7 boats
in this picture.